Mother Goose's
Playhouse

by Judy Sierra:

The Flannel Board Storytelling Book
Fantastic Theater
The Elephant's Wrestling Match
Cinderella
Goodnight Dinosaurs
Nursery Tales around the World

by Judy Sierra and Bob Kaminski:

Twice upon a Time
Multicultural Folktales

Mother Goose's Playhouse

Toddler tales and nursery rhymes
with patterns for puppets and feltboards

by

Judy Sierra

Bob Kaminski Media Arts

Book and cover design by Judy Sierra
Cover photo of Kosta Horaites by Bob Kaminski
Printed in the United States
Published by

    Bob Kaminski Media Arts
    183 Garfield Street
    Ashland, OR 97520
    (503) 482-1328

Library of Congress Cataloging in Publication Data:

Sierra, Judy
    Mother Goose's playhouse : toddler tales and nursery
rhymes, with patterns for puppets and feltboards / by
Judy Sierra.
      p.   cm.
   ISBN 0-9636089-1-6 : $14.95
   1. Storytelling.   2. Flannelgraphs.   3. Puppets.
I. Title.
LB1140.35.S76S54   1994
372.64'2--dc20
                                              93-35854
                                                  CIP

Contents

Sharing Rhymes and Stories
with Toddlers

This book is for parents, teachers and librarians who want to share literature with toddlers. One- to three-year-old children often have difficulty sitting still to listen to a nursery rhyme or a story. But just add a few feltboard characters or a puppet, and you will find that they are captivated. Not only do puppets and feltboards help young children make sense of the words they hear, but an exciting element of suspense and surprise is added as characters appear, move, and disappear during storytelling. Soon the children will begin saying the words along with you. Later they will demand to use these small theatrical props to recite the rhymes and tell the stories themselves.

On the pages that follow, you will find patterns for familiar nursery rhyme characters like Humpty Dumpty, Jack and Jill, and Little Bo Peep--and less familiar ones such as Giant Jim and Old Tom Turkey. The supplies you need to make feltboard figures, stick puppets, and puppet gloves are available at most fabric and craft stores (your scrap box may already contain everything you require). There is no machine sewing involved. Just use the recommended types of fabric and paper, along with glue, crayons, markers and fabric paint.

Children's involvement with these rhymes and stories can begin as they help you make the feltboard figures and puppets. Storytelling with feltboard and puppets is also an ideal way for older children to interact with a toddler. They can use their advanced skills of coloring and cutting, along with their knowledge of simple rhymes and tales, to teach and entertain their younger sisters and brothers.

When you are telling tales to toddlers, don't be afraid to ham it up as you chant the words, change your voice, and really sing out the rhymes. Literature must be a multi-sensory experience in order to appeal to young children. Be aware, however, that some toddlers are frightened by gruff voices or sudden changes in facial expression.

Try not to use a monotonous or singsong storytelling voice. Think about each rhyme or story, and tell it in a unique, creative way. When reciting "Hey, diddle diddle," will you add a barking laugh for the little dog? Why not make the word "moon" sound like a cow's long, soulful moo?

Don't be surprised if young children ask to hear the same rhyme or story many times. Saying a new rhyme three times in a row will not be too repetitious for a group of preschoolers. Let them know you're starting over by saying "Let's say that one again," or "I'm going to tell that one more time."

Toddlers' attention *will* wander away from you, especially when they are new to the experience of sitting and listening. Don't interpret this as a failure of your storytelling technique. Carry on with enthusiasm, and in time you will see your efforts rewarded.

If you're accustomed to telling stories to older children, you may be surprised when toddlers do not join you in saying repeated words and refrains. Toddlers do like to imitate simple sounds and large motions, and you can encourage this type of participation in a second or third telling, or in a separate activity following the storytelling.

Many of the rhymes in this book are also songs. Because they are folksongs, there is no one correct melody. The melody for any folksong will vary from singer to singer. When you want toddlers to sing along with you, it's best to use a simple melody within about a one-octave range. Toddler-friendly tunes for the rhymes in this book can be found in songbooks and on recordings such as the *Wee Sing* series, and those by Sharon, Lois, and Bram, and by Raffi.

How to Make a Feltboard

A feltboard (sometimes called a flannel board) is a rectangle of stiff cardboard covered with a fuzzy synthetic fabric. The feltboard provides a background for telling stories with moveable figures made of felt or interfacing. These figures cling to the upright feltboard because of the static electricity and friction between the fibers of the fabrics.

MATERIALS FOR MAKING A FELTBOARD

Artist's portfolio or rectangular
piece of cardboard

Synthetic fleece or velour fabric

White fabric glue

A feltboard may be as small as twelve by fifteen inches--a good size for a family or small daycare group. Librarians, nursery school teachers, and others who tell stories to large groups of children prefer a feltboard around eighteen inches high by twenty-four inches wide. The feltboard may be set upright on an easel, or it can be leaned against a wall or a chair back, with a slight slant back at the top. Feltboards are sold by school supply companies, but a homemade version is simple to make, costs less, and has the advantage that you can easily replace the fabric covering if it becomes worn or soiled.

A durable, portable feltboard may be made from a cardboard artist's portfolio, available in several useful sizes at artists' supply stores. Choose the type that has ribbon ties on three sides. Cut the covering fabric as large as one-half of the inside of the portfolio, and add one inch to each of the three outer sides. Apply fabric glue to the outer inch or so of the wrong side of the fabric. Match the fabric to the center fold of the portfolio, then overlap the three outer edges. When this feltboard is stored or carried, the fabric is well protected inside the portfolio. Opened, it sits nicely on a tabletop when you tie the two side ties loosely in half-bows.

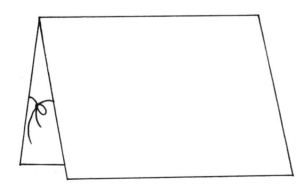

How to Make Feltboard Figures

Traceable patterns for feltboard figures are included in this book. These patterns have been drawn with both toddlers and storytellers in mind. Shapes that are easily recognized are best for young children. Storytellers need patterns that are fast and easy to color and cut out. If you need to make the patterns larger, use a photocopy machine that can enlarge images. One page of this book enlarged 129% will fill an eleven by seventeen inch sheet of paper.

Two types of fabric are used in making feltboard figures: colored felt and white interfacing (nonwoven, nonfusible).

Interfacing can be purchased by the yard at fabric stores, and is quite inexpensive. You can use it like paper, yet it is durable and clings to the feltboard. It is translucent, allowing you to trace the figures directly onto it from the pages of this book, or from a photocopy. Use any art medium that you would use on paper, from crayons, to watercolors, to markers (use a light touch with these). One preschool teacher I know colors the interfacing with permanent markers, then throws her feltboard figures in the washing machine when they become soiled. Artists' crayons and oil pastels are good choices if you enjoy blending colors. Although these will stain your hands as you use them, the color--surprisingly--will not rub off the figures later when you use them. Go over the outlines and interior lines of each figure with a fine tip, permanent black marker. Always cut out the figures *after* coloring.

Felt comes in a variety of shades, so you won't need to color it except to add details such as outlines and facial features. The felt sold in squares is better for this project than felt sold on bolts. The squares are stiffer and crisper. It's fun to decorate felt with the many types of fabric paints and glitter that come in squeeze tubes. Different colors of felt can be assembled collage-style, using fabric glue, to a backing of interfacing.

I use both felt and interfacing to make feltboard figures. I like to use interfacing for figures with a lot of detail, and felt for large figures, and for any figure that is mostly one color. Some storytellers use paper figures on the feltboard, but the figures in this book are designed to overlap and cling to each other in ways paper cannot.

MATERIALS FOR MAKING FELTBOARD FIGURES

Interfacing and
    crayons, oil pastels, or markers
    black fine-tip permanent marker

Colored felt squares and
    white fabric glue
    fabric paints (squeeze tubes)

Preschoolers can create their own feltboard figures. Provide them with felt cut into various shapes and sizes, a bit of white glue in a small dish, and a few nontoxic markers. Choose a rhyme for them to make that has just two or three characters such as "Little Miss Muffet" or "Old Tom Turkey." Often, the finished feltboard characters can only be identified by their child creators, but no matter. A child-size feltboard can be made by covering half the inside of a file folder with felt.

Storytelling with Feltboards

Arrange the feltboard pieces in the order you will use them before you begin. A glance at them will nudge your memory as the tale or rhyme unfolds. Hold the figures on your lap, or else place them out of sight on a tabletop behind the feltboard until it is time to use them. Specific suggestions for the placing of the figures are given with each rhyme or tale.

Rhymes and stories require different types of memory technique. Rhymes, like songs are learned word for word, while stories can be learned in outline and told in your own words (memorized stories sound stiff, and half the fun of storytelling is adding your own small personal touches). After learning a rhyme or story, practice telling it with the feltboard several times so that you know exactly when and where you want to place each figure. The placement of the figures is important because the rhymes and stories need to make sense visually. The more comfortable you are with placing the figures, the more freedom you have to interact creatively with your audience. Pausing before you add a new figure can bring suspense and enjoyment to the telling.

Making and Using Stick Puppets

Young children respond with delight to the simplest puppets. Stick puppets may be cut from construction paper and glued to craft sticks. Some of the rhymes have been designed especially for stick puppets, while most feltboard rhymes and stories can be adapted for stick puppet performance (by two or more puppeteers). Very durable stick puppets may be made by photocopying the patterns, coloring, and then laminating them.

MATERIALS FOR STICK PUPPETS

Construction paper or card stock
Crayons or markers
Craft sticks
Glue or clear tape

Finger Puppet Gloves

Rhymes in which characters appear and disappear one at a time can be presented in a charming way using simple flat figures attached to the fingertips of a glove.

Use a well-fitting glove of a dark or neutral color--a gardening glove is a good, inexpensive choice. Choose the glove, left or right, that you prefer to use in storytelling, and sew a half-inch circle of hook-and-loop tape (fuzzy side) to each fingertip of the glove, approximately on top of the fingernail. Position the hook-and-loop circle on the thumb carefully so that it will face the audience when you hold your hand up in a natural and relaxed way. Use heavy-duty thread or waxed dental floss to sew the hook-and-loop tape to the glove. A leather needle makes the job easier.

Like feltboard figures, the finger puppets may be made of either felt or interfacing. Complete the small figures, then glue each one to a duplicate shape cut from the rough hook side of the hook-and-loop tape. In this way, you can make several sets of detachable story figures to be used with one storytelling glove. Plastic wiggle-eyes enliven these little puppets. Some storytellers prefer to make the bodies of glove finger puppets from brightly colored acrylic pom poms (available at craft stores) with felt details glued on.

MATERIALS FOR A FINGER PUPPET GLOVE

Lightweight glove
2" wide hook-and-loop tape
Colored felt or interfacing
Fabric paint or markers
White fabric glue

Hey, diddle diddle

FELTBOARD

Hey, diddle diddle,

The cat and the fiddle,

The cow jumped over the moon.

The little dog laughed

To see such sport,

And the dish ran away with the

spoon.

FELTBOARD FIGURES. MOON, COW, CAT, DOG, DISH WITH SPOON.

STORYTELLING. BEGIN WITH THE CAT AND THE MOON ON THE FELTBOARD. LEAVE SPACE ABOVE THE MOON FOR THE COW. PLACE EACH FIGURE ON THE BOARD AS IT IS INTRODUCED IN THE RHYME.

Jack be nimble

STICK PUPPET

Jack be nimble,

Jack be quick,

Jack jump over the candlestick!

PUPPET & PROP. MAKE THE CANDLESTICK OUT OF CARDBOARD OR HEAVY PAPER.

STORYTELLING. HOLD THE CANDLESTICK IN ONE HAND AS YOU MOVE THE STICK PUPPET OF JACK BEHIND IT WITH THE OTHER.

Little Bo Peep

FELTBOARD

Little Bo Peep

Has lost her sheep,

And doesn't know where to find

    them.

Leave them alone,

And they'll come home,

Wagging their tails behind them.

FELTBOARD FIGURES. Bo Peep, sheep (make three), bushes (make two). The figures of Bo Peep and the bushes must conceal the sheep, so they should be made of felt.

STORYTELLING. Set up the feltboard before the children see it. Hide one sheep behind Little Bo Peep, the other two behind bushes, with the tips of their tails showing. None of the figures will be moved as you recite this rhyme. After you have finished, ask the children to help you find Little Bo Peep's sheep. The children can help you hide the sheep before you recite the rhyme again.

Humpty Dumpty

FELTBOARD

Humpty Dumpty sat on a wall.

Humpty Dumpty had a great fall.

All the king's horses

And all the king's men

Couldn't put Humpty Dumpty

together again.

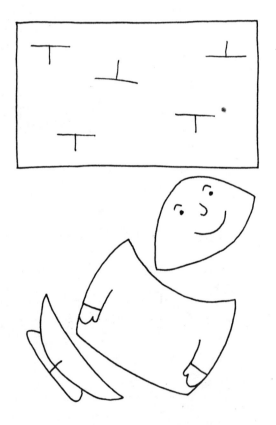

FELTBOARD FIGURES. HUMPTY DUMPTY, WALL, TWO HORSES, TWO MEN. MAKE HUMPTY DUMPTY FROM FELT, AND CUT HIM INTO PIECES--THREE PIECES, AS SHOWN, IS PLENTY FOR TODDLERS. YOU MAY WANT TO CUT HIM INTO SEVERAL JIGSAW-STYLE PIECES FOR OLDER CHILDREN. MAKE MORE HORSES AND MEN IF YOU WISH.

STORYTELLING. SET UP THE FELTBOARD BEFORE THE CHILDREN SEE IT. PLACE THE WALL AT THE CENTER, WITH HUMPTY DUMPTY ON TOP. WHEN HE HAS HIS FALL, PLACE THE PIECES AT THE BOTTOM OF THE FELTBOARD. ADD THE HORSES AND MEN AT EITHER SIDE OF THE FALLEN HUMPTY AS THEY ARE MENTIONED IN THE RHYME.

ASK THE CHILDREN TO HELP YOU PUT HUMPTY DUMPTY TOGETHER AGAIN. YOU MAY INVITE ONE OR TWO TO COME TO THE FELTBOARD TO HELP. IF YOU WANT THEM TO REMAIN SEATED, PUT THE PIECES TOGETHER YOURSELF (INCORRECTLY AT FIRST) AND ASK YOUR AUDIENCE IF YOU HAVE DONE IT RIGHT.

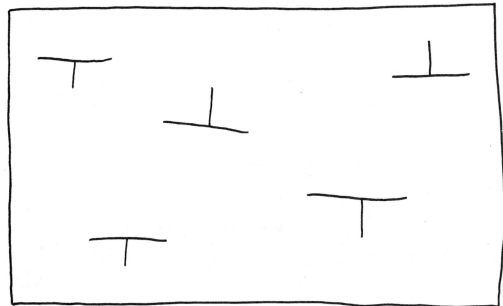

Little Miss Muffet

FELTBOARD

Little Miss Muffet

Sat on a tuffet,

Eating her curds and whey.

There came a big spider

Who sat down beside her,

And frightened Miss Muffet away.

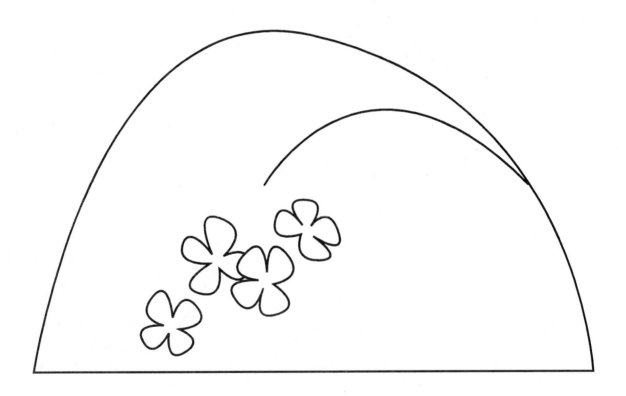

Pussycat, pussycat

FELTBOARD

Pussycat, pussycat, where have you
been?

I've been to London to visit the

queen.

Pussycat, pussycat, what did you
there?

I frightened a little mouse under the
chair.

FELTBOARD FIGURES. Queen, cat, mouse.

STORYTELLING. Begin the rhyme with just the cat on the feltboard. Add the queen, then the mouse, as each is mentioned. At the end, make the little mouse run away with a "squeak, squeak, squeak."

Bow wow says the dog

FELTBOARD

Bow wow, says the dog,

Mew mew, says the cat,

Oink oink, says the pig,

Squeak squeak, says the rat.

Too woo, says the owl,

Caw caw, says the crow,

Quack quack, says the duck,

Moooooooooooo, says the cow

FELTBOARD FIGURES. Dog, CAT, PIG, RAT, OWL, CROW, DUCK, COW.

STORYTELLING. You can either place each animal on the feltboard as you say its name, or else begin with all the animals on the feltboard, pointing to each one as you make its sound. When the children know the rhyme, pause before you say the name of each animal and give them an opportunity to say it.

Little Boy Blue

FELTBOARD

Little boy blue,

Come blow your horn.

The cow's in the meadow,

The sheep's in the corn.

But where is the little boy

Tending the sheep?

He's under the haystack

Fast asleep.

FELTBOARD FIGURES. LITTLE BOY BLUE, HAYSTACK, COW, SHEEP. THE HAYSTACK MUST CONCEAL LITTLE BOY BLUE, SO MAKE IT FROM FELT.

STORYTELLING. BEFORE THE CHILDREN SEE THE FELTBOARD, HIDE LITTLE BOY BLUE UNDER THE HAYSTACK WITH ONLY HIS FEET SHOWING. PLACE THE COW ON ONE SIDE OF THE HAYSTACK AND THE SHEEP ON THE OTHER. REMOVE THE COW, THEN THE SHEEP, WHEN THEY ARE MENTIONED IN THE RHYME. WHEN YOU FINISH, ASK THE CHILDREN TO HELP YOU FIND LITTLE BOY BLUE, THEN HAVE THEM MAKE A NOISE LIKE A HORN TO CALL BACK THE COW AND THE SHEEP.

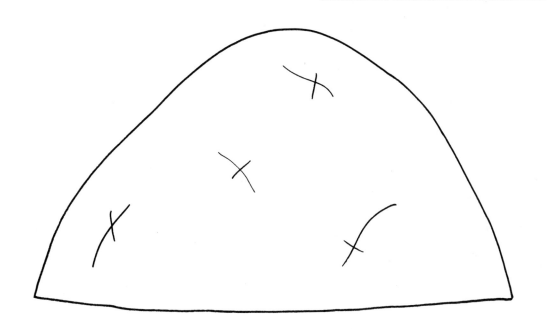

Dickery, dickery dare

FELTBOARD

Dickery, dickery dare,

A pig flew up in the air!

The man in brown

Soon brought him down,

Dickery, dickery dare.

FELTBOARD FIGURES. Pig, man, cloud.

STORYTELLING. Place the pig and the man near the bottom of the feltboard and the cloud at the top, then move the pig and the man up in the air and back down to the ground, following the sense of the rhyme.

Jack and Jill

FELTBOARD

Jack and Jill went up the hill

To fetch a pail of water.

Jack fell down

And broke his crown,

And Jill came tumbling after.

Up Jack got, and home did trot,

As fast as he could caper.

He went to bed

And fixed his head

With vinegar and brown paper.

FELTBOARD FIGURES. JACK, JILL, BED, BANDAGE. CUT A SIMPLE HILL SHAPE FROM BROWN OR GREEN FABRIC AND PIN IT TO THE FELTBOARD.

STORYTELLING. PLACE THE BED IN THE LOWER RIGHT CORNER OF THE FELTBOARD, AND JACK AND JILL IN LOWER LEFT. MOVE JACK AND JILL TO ILLUSTRATE THE STORY, ENDING WITH JACK IN BED WITH THE BANDAGE ON HIS HEAD.

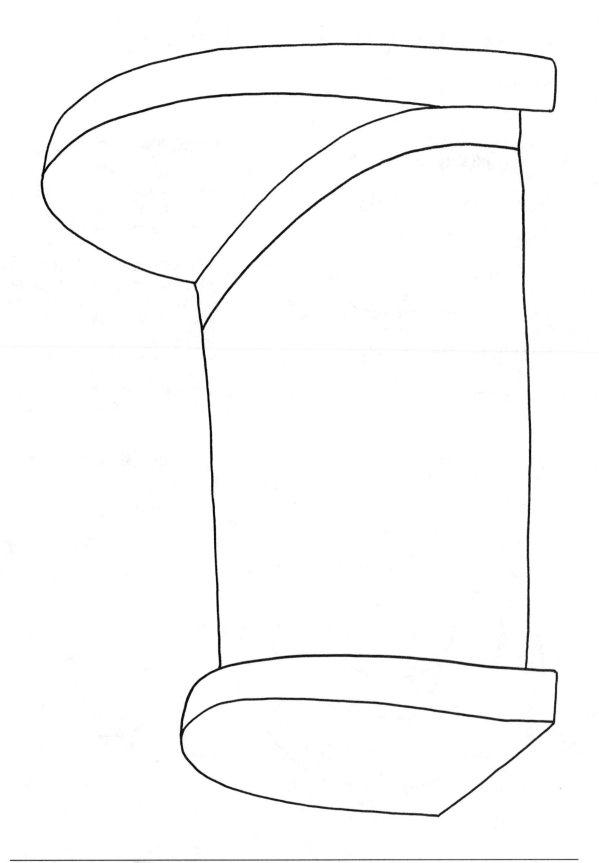

Hickety pickety, my black hen

FELTBOARD

Hickety pickety, my black hen,

She lays eggs for gentlemen.

Gentlemen come every day

To see what my black hen doth lay.

Sometimes nine and sometimes ten,

Hickety, pickety, my black hen.

FELTBOARD FIGURES. HEN, TWO GENTLEMEN, EGG (MAKE TEN). MAKE MORE GENTLEMEN IF YOU WISH.

STORYTELLING. PLACE THE HEN AT THE CENTER OF THE FELTBOARD. ADD A GENTLEMAN OR TWO TO EITHER SIDE OF HEN AS THEY ARE MENTIONED. AT THE END OF THE RHYME, SUGGEST TO THE CHILDREN THAT YOU COUNT THE NUMBER OF EGGS THE HEN HAS LAID TODAY. PLACE EITHER NINE OR TEN EGGS IN A ROW ACROSS THE BOTTOM OF THE FELTBOARD AND COUNT THEM.

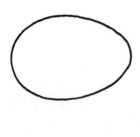

Rub a dub dub

FINGER PUPPET GLOVE

Rub a dub dub,

Three men in a tub,

And who do you think they be?

The butcher, the baker, the

    candlestick maker.

Throw them out, knaves all three!

PUPPETS & PROP. CUT THE TUB OUT OF CARDBOARD OR POSTER BOARD. ATTACH THE THREE FINGER PUPPETS TO THE INDEX, MIDDLE AND RING FINGERS OF A PUPPET GLOVE.

STORYTELLING. HOLD THE GLOVE IN FRONT OF YOU, PALM TOWARD YOUR CHEST, FINGERS TURNED DOWN. WITH YOUR OTHER HAND, HOLD THE TUB IN FRONT OF (TO THE AUDIENCE SIDE OF) YOUR GLOVED HAND. AS YOU SAY THE NAME OF EACH CHARACTER, HOLD UP THAT FINGER, SO THAT THE FINGER PUPPETS APPEAR IN THE TUB. ON THE WORDS "THROW THEM OUT . . ." BRING YOUR GLOVED HAND UP IN AN ARC SO THAT THE THREE MEN SEEM TO BE FLYING OUT OF THE TUB.

Baa baa, black sheep

FELTBOARD

Baa, baa, black sheep,

Have you any wool?

Yes, marry, have I,

Three bags full.

One for my master,

One for my dame,

One for the little boy

Who lives down the lane.

FELTBOARD FIGURES. SHEEP, THREE BAGS, MASTER, DAME, LITTLE BOY.

STORYTELLING. BEGIN THE RHYME WITH THE SHEEP IN AN UPPER CORNER OF THE FELTBOARD, AND THE THREE PEOPLE IN THE OPPOSITE LOWER CORNER. PLACE THE THREE BAGS NEXT TO THE SHEEP AS YOU MENTION THEM, THEN MOVE EACH BAG TO ITS NEW OWNER'S SIDE.

Hoddly poddly

FELTBOARD

Hoddly, poddly, puddles and fogs,

The cats are to marry the poodle dogs.

Cats in blue jackets and dogs in red

    hats,

What will become of the mice and

    the rats?

FELTBOARD FIGURES. CAT, DOG, MICE-AND-RATS. MAKE THE MICE-AND-RATS AS EITHER A FELTBOARD FIGURE OR A STICK PUPPET. MAKE AS MANY DOG-AND-CAT COUPLES AS YOU WISH.

STORYTELLING. PLACE THE CATS ON THE FELTBOARD BEFORE YOU BEGIN, THEN PLACE A POODLE BESIDE EACH CAT. AT THE END OF THE RHYME, EITHER PLACE A FELTBOARD FIGURE OF THE MICE-AND-RATS ON THE BOARD, OR MOVE A STICK PUPPET OF THEM ACROSS TOP EDGE OF THE FELTBOARD.

Giant Jim

FELTBOARD

The Giant Jim,

Great giant grim,

Wears a hat

Without a brim,

He's taller than

The tallest house,

But he trembles when

He meets a mouse.

FELTBOARD FIGURES. GIANT JIM, HOUSE, MOUSE. MAKE GIANT JIM OF FELT GLUED TO A BACKING OF INTERFACING. THIS WILL GIVE HIM ENOUGH STIFFNESS SO THAT YOU CAN LIFT HIM OFF THE FELTBOARD AT THE END OF THE RHYME. GIVE HIM A LITTLE SHAKE AND HE WILL SEEM TO TREMBLE.

STORYTELLING. BEGIN THE RHYME WITH BOTH GIANT JIM AND THE HOUSE ON THE FELTBOARD. FOR A LIVELY ENDING, MAKE THE MOUSE A FINGER PUPPET AND ATTACH IT TO THE FOREFINGER OF YOUR PUPPET GLOVE. HIDE THAT HAND UNTIL THE END OF THE RHYME. MAKE THE MOUSE SEEM TO RUN AT GIANT JIM. LIFT GIANT JIM--MAKE HIM TREMBLE, AND THEN DISAPPEAR.

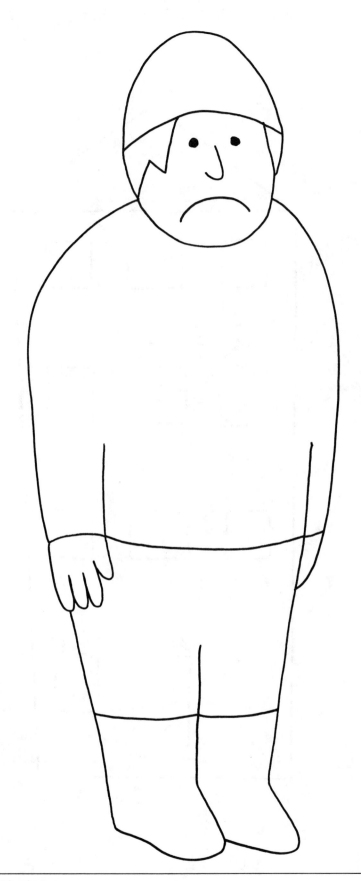

Old Tom Turkey

FELTBOARD

Old Tom Turkey lived on a hill,

--Gobble, gobble, gobble.

If he's not gone, he lives there still,

--Gobble, gobble, gobble.

A duck came by and said hello,

--Quack, quack, quack.

--Gobble, gobble, gobble.

Goodbye now, friend, it's time to go.

--Quack, quack, quack.

--Gobble, gobble, gobble.

FELTBOARD FIGURES. TURKEY, DUCK. CUT A HILL FROM BROWN OR GREEN FABRIC AND PIN IT TO THE FELTBOARD.

STORYTELLING. ADD SIMPLE BODY MOTIONS FOR CHILDREN TO IMITATE-- MOVE YOUR HEAD FROM SIDE TO SIDE WHILE YOU ARE SAYING "GOBBLE, GOBBLE, GOBBLE," AND FLAP YOUR ARMS WHEN YOU SAY "QUACK, QUACK, QUACK."

Mouse's Halloween house

by Judy Sierra

FELTBOARD

One day in the fall of the year, a little gray mouse found a big orange house. She nibbled a hole in the middle, to make a door. And she nibbled two holes up near the top, to make two windows. And then she nibbled a wide hole near the bottom, so that all her children could run in and out. Then she put a candle inside to light up the darkness.

The mouse's little house

Was a sight to be seen.

It was a jack-o'-lantern--

Happy Halloween!

FELTBOARD FIGURES. PUMPKIN, PUMPKIN'S TWO EYES, NOSE AND MOUTH, MOUSE, THREE MOUSE CHILDREN, CANDLE. CUT THE PUMPKIN OF ORANGE FELT, ITS EYES, NOSE AND MOUTH OF BLACK FELT.

STORYTELLING. USE PINS TO ATTACH THE PUMPKIN TO THE FELTBOARD. PLACE THE MOUSE NEXT TO IT. ADD THE PUMPKIN'S FEATURES AS YOU DESCRIBE THE MOUSE NIBBLING THE CORRESPONDING HOLES IN IT. PLACE THE MOUSE CHILDREN NEAR THE PUMPKIN'S MOUTH WHEN THEY ARE MENTIONED IN THE STORY.

The bear went over the mountain

STICK PUPPET

The bear went over the mountain,

The bear went over the mountain,

The bear went over the mountain,

To see what he could see.

But all he could see,

But all that he could see,

But all that he could see was . . .

The other side of the mountain

PUPPET & PROP. CUT A MOUNTAIN SHAPE FROM CARDBOARD ABOUT TWELVE INCHES HIGH AND COVER IT WITH FELT OR CONSTRUCTION PAPER. USING THE TWO BEAR PATTERNS, MAKE A TWO-SIDED PUPPET.

STORYTELLING. HOLD THE MOUNTAIN IN ONE HAND, AND THE BEAR PUPPET IN THE OTHER. MAKE THE BEAR APPEAR TO CLIMB UP THE MOUNTAIN, TURN AROUND, AND DESCEND.

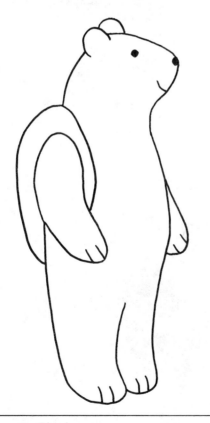 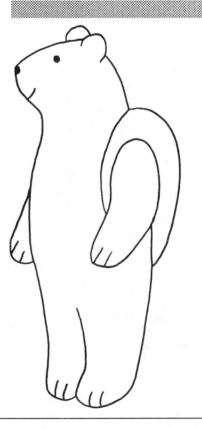

The itsy bitsy spider

FINGER PUPPET

The itsy bitsy spider

Climbed up the waterspout.

Down came the rain

And washed that spider out.

Out came the sun

And dried up all the rain.

Then the itsy bitsy spider

Climbed up the spout again.

PUPPET & PROPS. CUT A CIRCLE OF YELLOW CARDBOARD OR POSTER BOARD, ABOUT THREE OR FOUR INCHES IN DIAMETER, FOR THE SUN. ATTACH IT TO THE END OF A CHOPSTICK. CUT THIN STRIPS FROM A CLEAR PLASTIC BAG, ABOUT TWELVE INCHES LONG. TAPE THE ENDS OF THESE STRIPS TO ANOTHER CHOPSTICK TO MAKE THE RAIN.

STORYTELLING. ATTACH THE SPIDER FINGER PUPPET TO THE FOREFINGER OF YOUR PUPPET GLOVE, AND MIME ITS CLIMB UP AN IMAGINARY WATERSPOUT. USE THE RAIN AND SUN PROPS TO ACT OUT THE RHYME.

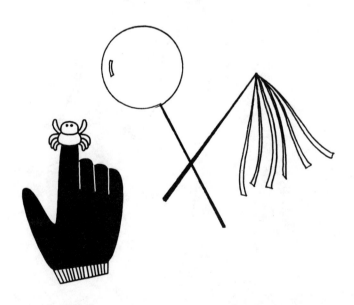

Teddy wore his red shirt

Teddy wore his red shirt, red shirt, red shirt,
Teddy wore his red shirt all day long.

Teddy wore his blue pants, blue pants, blue pants,
Teddy wore his blue pants all day long.

Teddy wore his yellow hat, yellow hat, yellow hat,
Teddy wore his yellow hat all day long.

Teddy wore his green socks, green socks, green socks,
Teddy wore his green socks all day long.

Teddy wore his white shoes, white shoes, white shoes,
Teddy wore his white shoes all day long.

(This can be sung to the tune of "Mary wore her red dress.")

FELTBOARD FIGURES. TEDDY BEAR, SHIRT, PANTS, SOCKS, SHOES, HAT. ALL THESE FIGURES SHOULD BE CUT FROM FELT.

STORYTELLING. ATTACH THE BEAR TO THE FELTBOARD WITH PINS, AND SET HIS CLOTHING AROUND HIM. AS YOU SAY THE RHYME, PLACE HIS CLOTHING ON HIM. CHILDREN CAN HELP YOU BY POINTING TO THE CLOTHES AS YOU NAME THEM.

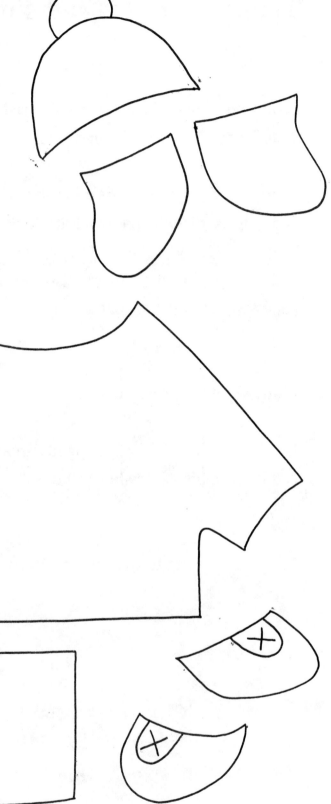

A-hunting we will go

FELTBOARD

A-hunting we will go, a-hunting we will go,

We'll catch a fox and put him in a box,

And then we'll let him go.

A-hunting we will go, a-hunting we will go,

We'll catch a bear and comb her hair,

And then we'll let her go.

A-hunting we will go, a-hunting we will go,

We'll catch a mouse and put him in a house,

And then we'll let him go.

A-hunting we will go, a-hunting we will go,

We'll catch a whale and tickle her tail,

And then we'll let her go.

A-hunting we will go, a-hunting we will go,

We'll catch a goat and put him in a boat,

And then we'll let him go.

FELTBOARD FIGURES. Fox, box, bear, mouse, house, whale, goat, boat.

STORYTELLING. Place the figures on the feltboard as they are mentioned and remove them after the words "let him/her go." Pantomime combing the bear's hair and tickling the whale's tail. Older children will enjoy creating new verses and feltboard figures for this rhyme.

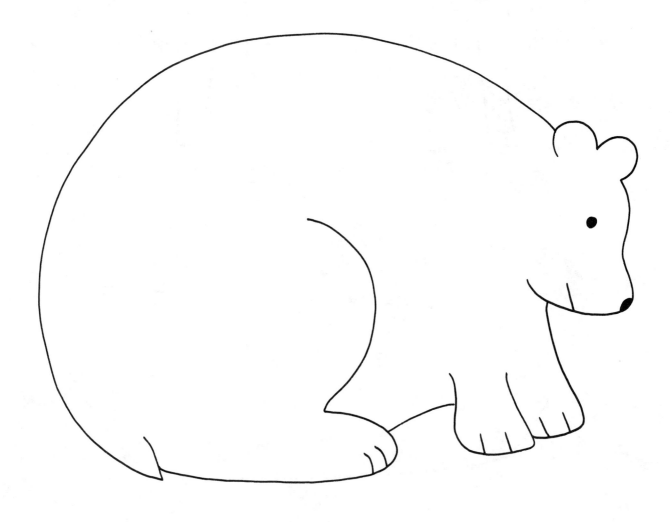

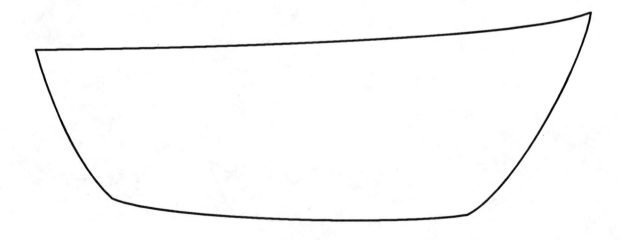

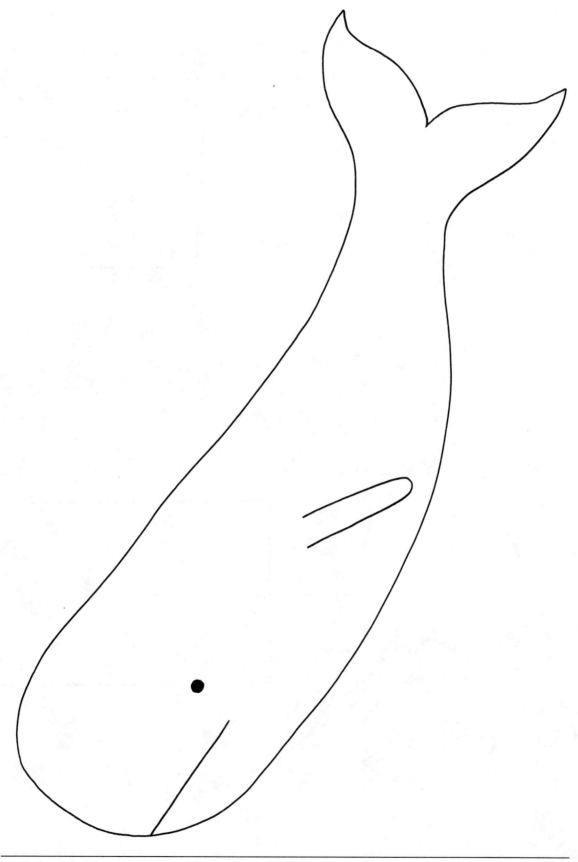

Mother Goose's Playhouse

Five little ducks

FINGER PUPPET GLOVE

Five little ducks went out to play,
Over the hills and far away.
When mother duck said,
Quack, quack, quack!
Only four little ducks came back.

Four little ducks went out to play,
Over the hills and far away.
When mother duck said,
Quack, quack, quack!
Only three little ducks came back.

Three little ducks went out to play,
Over the hills and far away.
When mother duck said,
Quack, quack, quack!
Only two little ducks came back.

Two little ducks went out to play,
Over the hills and far away.
When mother duck said,
Quack, quack, quack!
Only one little duck came back.

One little duck went out to play,

Over the hills and far away.

When mother duck said,

QUACK! QUACK! QUACK!

Five little ducks came running back.

PUPPETS. MAKE FIVE DUCK FINGER PUPPETS, THREE FACING ONE DIRECTION AND TWO THE OTHER.

STORYTELLING. YOU WILL PLAY THE PART OF THE MOTHER DUCK (OR FATHER DUCK, IN WHICH CASE YOU WILL CHANGE THE WORDS). WITH EACH VERSE, MAKE THE LITTLE DUCKS APPEAR TO RUN AWAY FROM YOU AND THEN RUN BACK.

AFTER EACH OF THE FIRST FOUR "QUACK-QUACK-QUACKS," ONE LITTLE DUCK DISAPPEARS AS YOU FOLD ONE FINGER AT A TIME TOWARD YOUR PALM-- FIRST THE THUMB, THEN THE LITTLE FINGER (HOLD IT DOWN WITH YOUR THUMB), THEN THE RING FINGER, AND SO ON. MAKE THE MOTHER DUCK'S FINAL "QUACK-QUACK- QUACK" LOUDER AND LONGER. PAUSE FOR A MOMENT AND THEN OPEN YOUR HAND QUICKLY AS YOU MAKE ALL FIVE LITTLE DUCKS RESPOND OBEDIENTLY AND COME RUNNING BACK.

Five little monkeys

FINGER PUPPET GLOVE

There were five little monkeys jumping on the bed;
One fell off and bumped her head.
Mama called the doctor and the doctor said,
"No more monkeys jumping on that bed!"

There were four little monkeys jumping on the bed;
One fell off and bumped her head.
Mama called the doctor and the doctor said,
"No more monkeys jumping on that bed!"

There were three little monkeys jumping on the bed;
One fell off and bumped her head.
Mama called the doctor and the doctor said,
"No more monkeys jumping on that bed!"

There were two little monkeys jumping on the bed;
One fell off and bumped her head.
Mama called the doctor and the doctor said,
"No more monkeys jumping on that bed!"

There was one little monkey jumping on the bed;

She fell off and bumped her head.

Mama called the doctor and the doctor said,

"No more monkeys jumping on that bed!"

Five little speckled frogs

FINGER PUPPET GLOVE

Five little speckled frogs sat on a speckled log

Eating some most delicious bugs (*yum, yum*).

One jumped into the pool

Where it was nice and cool,

Then there were four speckled frogs.

Four little speckled frogs sat on a speckled log

Eating some most delicious bugs (*yum, yum*).

One jumped into the pool

Where it was nice and cool,

Then there were three speckled frogs.

Three little speckled frogs sat on a speckled log

Eating some most delicious bugs (*yum, yum*).

One jumped into the pool

Where it was nice and cool,

Then there were two speckled frogs.

Two little speckled frogs sat on a speckled log

Eating some most delicious bugs (*yum, yum*).

One jumped into the pool

Where it was nice and cool,

Then there was one speckled frog.

One little speckled frog sat on a speckled log

Eating some most delicious bugs (*yum, yum*).

He jumped into the pool

Where it was nice and cool,

Then there were no speckled frogs *(boo hoo)*.

PUPPETS & PROP. ADJUST THE OUTLINE OF THE LOG PATTERN BEFORE YOU CUT IT OUT SO THAT WHEN YOU HOLD YOUR PUPPET GLOVE BEHIND IT, THE FIVE FROGS APPEAR TO BE SITTING ON TOP OF IT.

STORYTELLING. TELL THE STORY HOLDING THE LOG IN ONE HAND WITH YOUR PUPPET GLOVE BEHIND IT. AS EACH FROG "JUMPS INTO THE POOL," FOLD DOWN ONE FINGER--FIRST YOUR THUMB, THEN LITTLE FINGER (HOLD IT DOWN WITH YOUR THUMB), THEN THE RING FINGER, ETC.

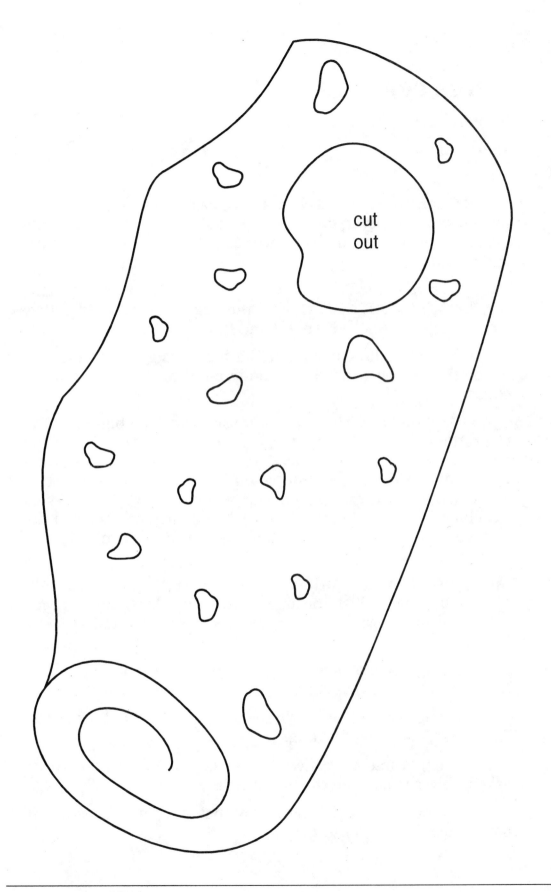

cut
out

Three eggs in a basket

by Judy Sierra

FELTBOARD

Once, three eggs lay in a tiny basket. One looked just like an ordinary, everyday egg. One looked just the same, only bigger. The third egg looked different. It was small, and white, and round.

Tap, tap, tap. There was a noise inside the first egg. *Tap, tap, tap. TAP, TAP, TAP.* Out of the egg came a fluffy yellow chick. The chick walked around and fluffed its feathers.

The litte chick looked at the bigger egg. What could be inside that big egg, the chick wondered. It must be a big fluffy chick!

Tap, tap, tap. There was a noise inside the big egg. The egg rattled, and rolled. *Tap, tap, tap. TAP, TAP, TAP.* Out of the egg came a fuzzy yellow duckling. The chick and the duckling looked at the third egg. Who could be inside, they wondered. The chick touched the egg with its beak. "This egg is soft," said the chick. "I don't think it will hatch." The duckling touched the egg with its bill. "This egg is cold," said the duckling. "I don't think it will hatch."

Just then, the little egg wiggled, and rolled, and split open. Out came a little head, and two little legs, and a green shell, and two more little legs, and a short pointy tail. It was a baby turtle!

Along came a hen. "Where is my baby?" the hen asked. "Here I am," said the chick.

Along came a duck. "Where is my baby?" the duck asked. "Here I am," said the duckling.

Along came a turtle. "Where is *my* baby?" the turtle asked. "Here I am," said the little turtle.

The eggs in the basket had all hatched, and three happy babies found their mothers.

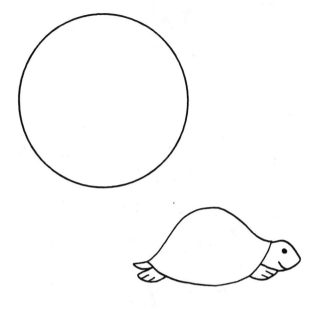

FELTBOARD FIGURES. Basket, chick, duckling, baby turtle, three eggs, hen, duck, turtle. Cut the eggs from felt so that they will conceal the babies underneath. Make the baby animals from interfacing.

STORYTELLING. Set up the feltboard before the children see it, with the three baby animals hidden under the three eggs. As each egg hatches, take the baby from beneath it and place it beside the basket. When each mother (or father) appears place the proper baby by its side

The little house

(adapted from a Russian tale)

FELTBOARD

One day, Gray Mouse was running through a meadow looking for seeds to eat, and what did he find? A little house! "This will make a good house for me," said the mouse. He went up to the door. "Little house, little house," called Gray Mouse, "who lives in this little house?" No one answered. There was no one inside. Gray Mouse moved in. He swept the floor, and made a nice home.

Along came Croaking Frog, jumping and leaping. When he saw the house, he went up to the door and called out, "Little house, little house, who lives in this little house?" From inside the little house, a voice answered, "I am Gray Mouse, who are you?" "I am Croaking Frog. May I come live with you?" "Yes! Come in. Make yourself at home," said Gray Mouse. So Croaking Frog went inside, and they lived together.

Along came Hoppity Hare, running and bouncing. When she saw the house, she went to the door and called out, "Little house, little house, who lives in the little house?" From inside two friends answered, "We do, Gray Mouse and Croaking Frog. Who are you?" "I am Hoppity Hare. May I come live with you?" "Yes! Come in. Make yourself at home," said Gray Mouse and Croaking Frog. So Hoppity Hare went inside, and they all lived together.

Along came Lickity Fox, skipping and prancing. When she saw the house, she went to the door and called out, "Little house, little house, who lives in the little house?" From inside three friends answered, "We do, Gray Mouse, Croaking Frog, and Hoppity Hare. Who are you?" "I am Lickity Fox. May I come live with you?" "Yes! Come in. Make yourself at home," said Gray Mouse, Croaking Frog, and Hoppity Hare." So Lickity Fox went inside, and they all lived together.

Along came Bear Sqaush-a-Lot, sniffing and snooping. When he saw the little house, he went to the door and called out "Little house, little house, who lives in the little house?" From inside the four friends answered, "We do, Gray Mouse, Croaking Frog, Hoppity Hare, and Lickity Fox. Who are you?" "I am Bear Squash-a-Lot, and I want to live with you in the little house."

"No, no, you can't. You'll break our little house and squash us all!" cried Gray Mouse, Croaking Frog, Hoppity Hare, and Lickity Fox. Bear Squash-a-Lot stuck his nose into the little house and said, "Here I come!"

Crick-crack! The little house fell down. Out jumped Lickity Fox, "Little house is broken," she said, and ran away. Out jumped Hoppity Hare, "Little house is smashed," she said, and ran away. Out jumped Croaking Frog, "Little house is ruined," he said, and ran away. Out jumped Gray Mouse, "Little house is squashed," he said, and ran away

Bear Squash-a-Lot grumbled, "I don't like that house," and stomped away. That was the end of the little house.

FELTBOARD FIGURES. Mouse, frog, hare, fox, bear. Make the house from two rectangles of felt, a light on top of a dark color. Cut a peaked roof. Glue or sew the two felt pieces on the dotted lines as indicated. Place a pipe cleaner in the roof with a hook protruding at the peak to hang the house on the top of the felt-board. Cut a door and four windows in the top felt only. Mark and cut the windows so the face of each animal will show when you slip it in the open slot at the side of the house. Make the animals from either heavy paper, or from felt or inter-facing glued to heavy paper. This will make them stiff enough to slide easily into the slots.

STORYTELLING. Attach the lit-tle house to the feltboard, using the pipe-cleaner hook. Hold each animal as it asks who lives in the little house, then slide it into its slot in the side of the house. When Bear Squash-a-Lot tries to get in, lift the house off the feltboard and have it col-lapse onto the tabletop or onto your lap. Then pick up each animal in turn and hold it up for the children to see as it speaks, then runs away.

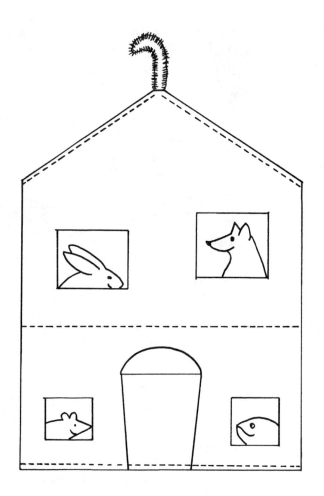

The giant carrot

(adapted from a Russian tale)

FELTBOARD

Once a rabbit was hopping through the garden when she came upon a green carrot top. The carrot top was especially big, and the little rabbit said, "This must be a GIANT carrot!" The rabbit held onto the carrot top and pulled--*mruff*--and pulled--*mruff*--and pulled--*mruff!* But the carrot wouldn't come out.

Along came a squirrel and asked what was the matter. The rabbit said, "This carrot won't come out!" So the squirrel said, "Let me help." The squirrel held onto the rabbit, and the rabbit held onto the carrot top and they pulled-- *mruff*--and pulled--*mruff*--and pulled--*mruff!* But the carrot wouldn't come out.

Along came a turtle and asked what was the matter. The squirrel said, "This carrot won't come out!" So the turtle said, "Let me help." The turtle held onto the squirrel, and the squirrel held onto the rabbit, and rabbit held onto to the carrot top and together they pulled--*mruff*--and pulled--*mruff*--and pulled--*mruff!* But that carrot wouldn't come out.

Along came a snail and asked what was the matter. The turtle said, "This carrot won't come out!" The snail said, "Let me help." The turtle, and the squirrel, and the rabbit just laughed at the snail. "You're too small," they said. But the snail said, "I CAN help. Let me try." So the snail held onto the turtle, and the turtle held onto the squirrel, and the squirrel held onto the rabbit, and the rabbit held onto to the carrot top. And together they pulled--*mruff*--and pulled--*mruff*--and pulled--*mruff!* And that carrot DID come out. And it was a GIANT carrot. And the rabbit and the squirrel and the turtle and the snail ate up every last bit.

FELTBOARD FIGURES. CARROT, RABBIT, SQUIRREL, TURTLE, SNAIL. USE FELT TO MAKE A HILL AT LEAST AS HIGH AS THE CARROT IS LONG.

STORYTELLING. SET UP THE FELTBOARD BEFORE THE CHILDREN SEE IT. PLACE THE CARROT UNDER THE HILL SO THAT THE BASE OF THE CARROT'S LEAVES IS AT THE TOP OF THE HILL. PIN THE HILL TO THE FELTBOARD, MAKING SURE THAT YOU WILL BE ABLE TO PULL THE CARROT UP AND OUT AT THE END OF THE STORY. PLACE EACH ANIMAL ON THE HILL AS IT APPEARS IN THE STORY, ONE BEHIND THE OTHER. THE SOUND "MRUFF" CAN BE CHANGED TO YOUR FAVORITE PULLING SOUND. MIME A PULLING MOTION AS YOU SAY IT.

Mother Goose's Playhouse

7459